D1439413

MANCHESTER
CITY COUNCIL

Please return/renew this item
by the last date shown.
Books may also be renewed by
phone or the internet.

Tel: 0161 254 7777

www.manchester.gov.uk/libraries

STER!
STY!
iNK!

BLOOMSBURY CHILDREN'S BOOKS
Bloomsbury Publishing Plc
50 Bedford Square, London, WC1B 3DP, UK
29 Earlsfort Terrace, Dublin 2, Ireland

BLOOMSBURY, BLOOMSBURY CHILDREN'S BOOKS and the Diana logo are trademarks of Bloomsbury Publishing Plc
First published in Great Britain 2023 by Bloomsbury Publishing Plc

A catalogue record for this book is available from the British Library

ISBN 978 1 5266 0681 5 (HB)
ISBN 978 1 5266 0683 9 (PB)
ISBN 978 1 5266 0682 2 (eBook)

1 3 5 7 9 10 8 6 4 2

Printed and bound in China by Leo Paper Products, Heshan, Guangdong

MIX
Paper from
responsible sources
FSC
www.fsc.org
FSC® C020056

To find out more about our authors and books visit www.bloomsbury.com and sign up for our newsletters

For Rafa, who wanted to watch me write this story . . .
and made some clever suggestions – S.T.

For Matteo, Salomé, Joachim,
my little monsters who thirst for life! – F.B.

MONSTER! THIRSTY! DRINK!

BLOOMSBURY
CHILDREN'S BOOKS
LONDON OXFORD NEW YORK NEW DELHI SYDNEY

Sean Taylor

Fred Benaglia

THiRSTY!

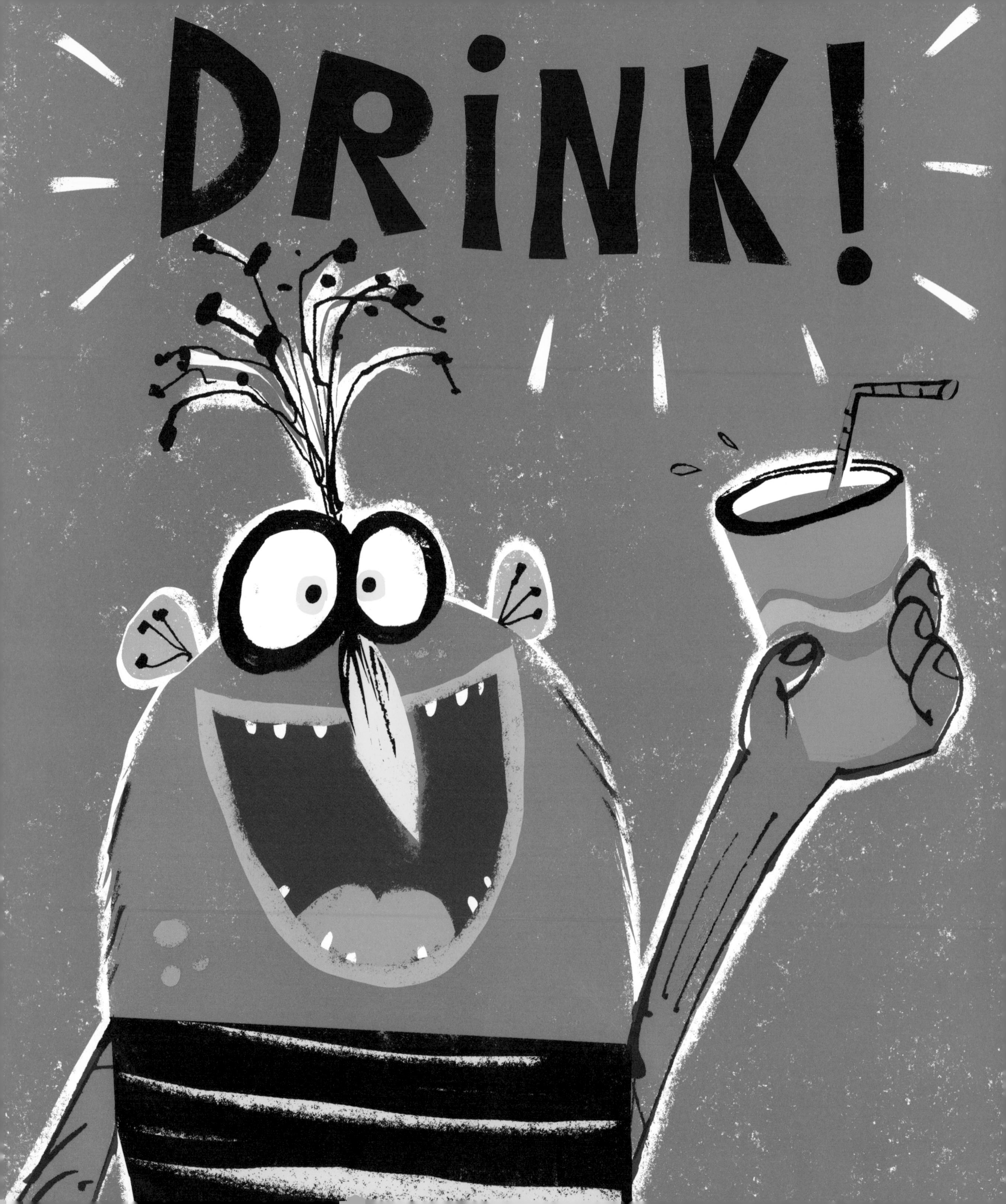
DRINK!

MONSTER! THIRSTY!

OH ME OH MY!

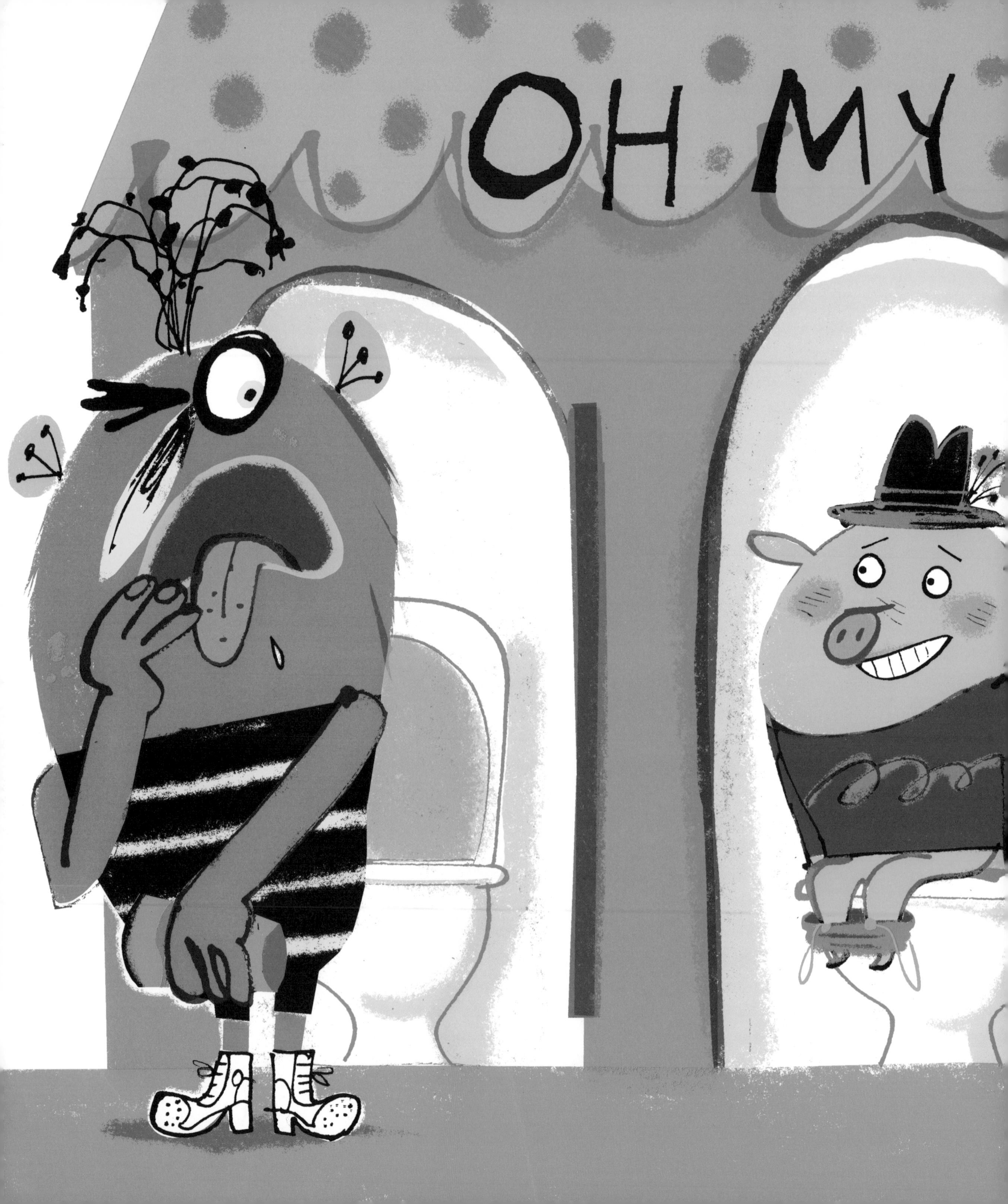
OH MY

MONSTER...

THIRSTY!

SLURP!

MONSTER! BURSTING!

TOILETS

CLOSED
FOR
CLEANING